Love yourself
as you are!

Geoffrey Frost

Written for my first son, Liam.

ZEE

The Envious
Zebra

Once upon a time there was a young zebra named Zee. Like other young zebras, he loved to spend his days running and playing with his friends on the African savannah. He was a confident, but naive little zebra

and one strange thing – he had never really looked at himself before!

One day, while drinking from the local water hole, Zee looked into the water and saw his reflection....

"What is THAT?" asked Zee

"THAT is YOU, silly zebra" said an old monkey

So young Zee went running off, full of self-confidence – but every once in a while he would think about what the old monkey had said – and one day he saw a creature that he had never seen before.......

Wow!

"Look at those beautiful feathers!" thought Zee" I've never seen such beautiful colors – and all I have are these boring black and white stripes!"

So little Zee became sad, because he thought that the peacock was more beautiful than he was...

The more he thought of it, the sadder he became - but being a resourceful little zebra, he decided to ask the peacock where he got his feathers, so that he could get some too.

"Excuse me, Mr. Bird" said Zee "but, um, your feathers are very beautiful and I was wondering where you got them?"

"What a question! Why young zebra, I may as well ask you where you got your stripes!! Why, we have both been gifted by Allah, our creator, though creatures here call him Obatala, or sometimes Papa Oba."

"Hmmph! Well let me tell you Mr. Bird, I think it's unfair! I want beautiful feathers too! And I'm going to demand that Allah, or Oba or whoever give me some!" said Zee

Before the peacock could say a word, Zee galloped away, intending to give the creator a piece of his mind, until he realized...

...he had forgotten to ask the bird where the creator lived!!

"Then stand still while I eat you you stupid zebra! You will find him in my belly!!" growled the leopard.

With a tremendous roar the leopard lashed out with his claws! Zee just managed to get out of reach in time, and he ran as fast and as far as his legs would take him!!

"Well as far as I know, Zebra, he likes to sleep in the sky – so I imagine if you climb to the top of the mountain and call out his name – (I know him as God but creatures around here call him Papa Oba) he should answer you. But what do you want to see him for?" asked the old turtle.

So Zee told him all about what had happened and what he wanted from the creator – sharp claws and a spotted coat and peacock feathers...

"I think I'll ask him for a shell like yours, too, turtle, because I know it protects you <u>really well!</u>" added Zee

"Oh Zebra" said the old turtle "I don't think you should bother him with that!

God made you just the way you were supposed to be!"

Now all this talk about the creator had awakened Papa Oba from his nap in the clouds. "Who keeps on calling my name?" he thought.

Looking down from the clouds, Oba saw Zee climbing and struggling to reach the top of the mountain. Instantly, Obatala knew the whole story.

"Bah! It's that ungrateful zebra Zee! I know just what he wants. Well, come let him ask - I will teach that zebra a lesson!"

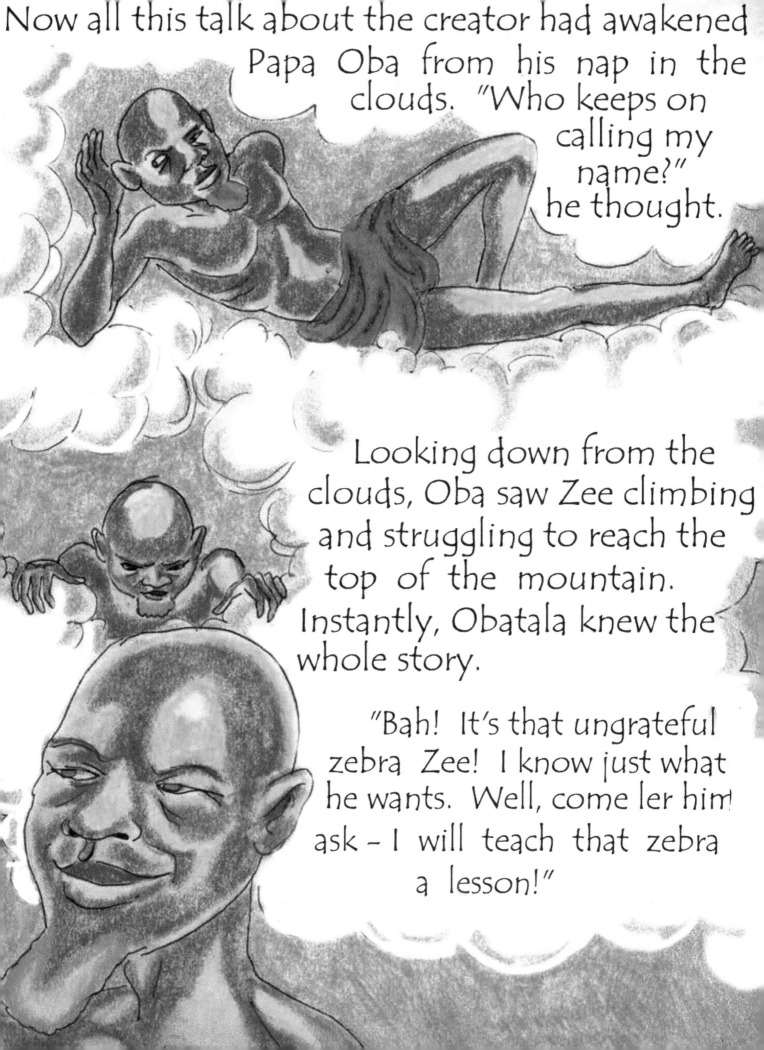

Shaking his head with dissappointment with Zee's rude and demanding tone, Obatala reached down from the sky and touched Zee with the power of his smallest finger.

"Your wish is graciously granted."

said Papa Oba.

And what a a monstrous, ridiculous creature Zee had become!

A zebra - headed, leopard - skinned, peacock - tailed, turtle - thing!!

And yet, Zee was happy! He had received all he had asked for! "No one in the savannah has ever seen as fantastic a creature as I!" he thought "Wait until my friends see me! Wait until that leopard sees me!!"

So Zee trundled down the mountain as fast as he could and soon he reached the very same spot where the leopard slept...

But when his friends saw him coming through the tall grass, they winnied and screamed: "RUN! RUN! It's a monster!! RUN ! RUN!"

"Wait! Wait! It's me, Zee!" he called, but it was too late. They had run away...

and Zee was lonely, and sad.

But Zee was a resourceful little zebra, and he thought, "I know! I'm part turtle now—I'll go play with the turtles!"

But when he came to where the turtles lived, they all hid in their shells, and no matter what Zee said, they would not come out.

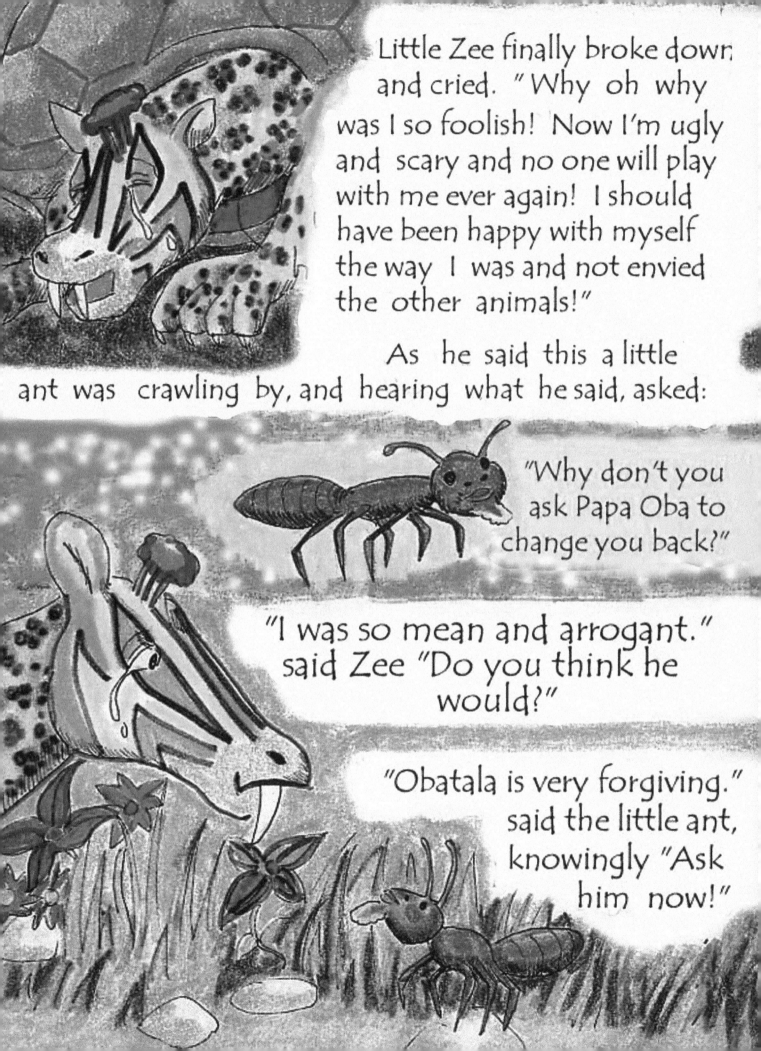

Little Zee finally broke down and cried. "Why oh why was I so foolish! Now I'm ugly and scary and no one will play with me ever again! I should have been happy with myself the way I was and not envied the other animals!"

As he said this a little ant was crawling by, and hearing what he said, asked:

"Why don't you ask Papa Oba to change you back?"

"I was so mean and arrogant." said Zee "Do you think he would?"

"Obatala is very forgiving." said the little ant, knowingly "Ask him now!"

CPSIA information can be obtained
at www.ICGtesting.com
Printed in the USA
BVHW021310031221
623170BV00015B/598